THE COMPLETE
FARMYARD TALES

Heather Amery
Illustrated by Stephen Cartwright

Language Consultant: Betty Root
Reading and Language Information Centre
University of Reading, England

There is a little yellow duck to find on every page.

Notes for Parents

The stories in this delightful picture book are ones which your child will want to share with you many times.

All the stories in *Farmyard Tales* have been written in a special way to ensure that young children succeed in their first efforts to read.

To help with that success, first read the whole of one story aloud and talk about the pictures. Then encourage your child to read the short, simpler text at the top of each page and read the longer text at the bottom of the page yourself. This "turn about" reading builds up confidence and children do love joining in. It is a great day when they discover that they can read a whole story for themselves.

Farmyard Tales provides an enjoyable opportunity for parents and children to share the excitement of learning to read.

Betty Root

PIG GETS STUCK

This is Apple Tree Farm.

This is Mrs Boot, the farmer. She has two children called Poppy and Sam, and a dog called Rusty.

2

On the farm there are six pigs.

The pigs live in a pen with a little house.
The smallest pig is called Curly.

It is time for breakfast.

Mrs Boot gives the pigs their breakfast.
But Curly is so small, he does not get any.

Curly is hungry.

He walks round the pen looking for something to eat. Then he finds a little gap under the wire.

Curly is out.

He squeezes through the gap under the wire.
He is out in the farmyard.

6

He walks round the farmyard, looking at the
animals. Which breakfast would he like to eat?

7

Curly wants the hens' breakfast.

He thinks the hens' breakfast looks good.
He squeezes through the gap in the fence.

8

Curly tries it.

He eats some of the hens' food. It is so good he gobbles it all up. The hens are cross.

Mrs Boot sees Curly.

Curly hears Mrs Boot shouting at him.
"What are you doing in the hen run, Curly?"

He runs to the fence.

He tries to squeeze through the gap. But he has eaten so much breakfast, he is too fat.

11

Curly pushes and pushes but he can't move.
He is stuck in the fence.

12

They all push.

Mrs Boot, Poppy and Sam all push Curly.
He squeals and squeals. His sides hurt.

13

Curly is out.

Then, with a grunt, Curly pops through the
fence. "He's out, he's out," shouts Sam.

14

He is safe now.

Mrs Boot picks up Curly. "Poor little pig," she says. And she carries him back to the pig pen.

Curly is happy.

"Tomorrow you shall have lots of breakfast," she says. And Curly was never, ever hungry again.

THE NAUGHTY SHEEP

This is Apple Tree Farm.

This is Mrs Boot, the farmer. She has two children
called Poppy and Sam. And a dog called Rusty.
18

On the farm there are seven sheep.

The sheep live in a big field with a fence round it.
One sheep has a black eye. She is called Woolly.

Woolly is bored.

Woolly stops eating and looks over the fence.
"Grass," she says, "nothing but grass. Boring."

Woolly runs out of the gate.

She runs out of the field into the farmyard.
Then she runs through another gate into a garden.

21

Woolly sees lots to eat in the garden.

She tastes some of the flowers. "Very good,"
she says, "and much prettier than grass."
22

Can you see where Woolly walked?

She walks round the garden, eating lots of the flowers. "I like flowers," she says.

23

Mrs Boot sees Woolly in the garden.

"What are you doing in my garden?" she shouts.
"You've eaten my flowers, you naughty sheep."

Mrs Boot is very cross.

"It's the Show today," she says. "I was going to pick my best flowers for it. Just look at them."

It is time for the Show.

"Come on," says Poppy "We must go now. The Show starts soon. It's only just down the road."
26

They all walk down the road.

Woolly watches them go. She chews her flower and thinks, "I'd like to go to the Show."

Woolly goes to the Show.

Woolly runs down the road. Soon she comes to a
big field with lots of people in it.

Woolly goes into the ring.

She pushes past the people and into the field.
She stops by a man in a white coat.

29

Mrs Boot finds her.

"What are you doing here, Woolly?" says Mrs Boot.
"She has just won a prize," says the man.

Woolly is the winner.

"This cup is for the best sheep," says the man.
"Oh, that's lovely. Thank you," says Mrs Boot.

It is time to go home.

"Come on, Woolly," says Mrs Boot. "We'll take you back to your field, you naughty, clever sheep."

BARN ON FIRE

This is Apple Tree Farm

Mrs Boot is the farmer. She has two children
called Poppy and Sam, and a dog called Rusty.
34

This is Ted.

Ted works at Apple Tree Farm. He looks after the tractor and all the other farm machines.

Poppy and Sam help Ted.

They like helping Ted with jobs on the farm.
Today he is mending the fence round the sheep field.

Sam smells smoke.

"Ted," says Sam, "I think something's burning."
Ted stops working and they all sniff hard.

The barn is on fire.

"Look," says Poppy, "there's smoke coming from the hay barn. It must be on fire. What shall we do?"

38

"Call the fire brigade."

"Come on," says Ted. "Run to the house and tell your Mum to call the fire brigade. Run as fast as you can."

Poppy and Sam run to the house.

"Mum, Mum," shouts Poppy. "Call the fire brigade."
"The hay barn is on fire. Quickly, Mum."

40

Mrs Boot dials the number.

"It's Apple Tree Farm." she says. "The fire brigade, please, as fast as you can. Thank you very much."

41

"You must stay here."

"Now, Poppy," says Mrs Boot. "I want you and Sam to stay indoors. And don't let Rusty out."

42

Poppy and Sam watch from the door.

Soon they hear the siren. Then the fire engine roars up the road and into the farmyard.

"The firemen are here."

The firemen jump down from the engine. They lift down lots of hoses and unroll them.

44

The firemen run toward the barn with the hoses.
Can you see where they get the water from?

The firemen squirt water on to the barn.

Poppy and Sam watch them from the window.
"It's still burning on the other side," says Poppy.

"There's the fire."

One fireman runs round the barn. What a surprise!
Two campers are cooking on a big wood fire.

The fire is out.

"We're sorry," say the campers. "It was exciting," says Sam, "but I'm glad the barn is all right."

THE RUNAWAY TRACTOR

This is Apple Tree Farm.

Mrs Boot is the farmer. She has two children
called Poppy and Sam, and a dog called Rusty.

Ted is the tractor driver.

He has filled the trailer with hay. He is taking
it to the fields to feed the sheep.

Poppy and Sam hear a funny noise.

"Listen," says Sam. "Ted is shouting and the tractor is making a funny noise. Let's go and look."
52

They run to the top of the hill.

The tractor is racing down the hill, going faster and faster. "It won't stop," shouts Ted.

The trailer comes off.

The trailer runs down the hill and crashes into a fence. It tips up and all the hay falls out.

The tractor runs into the pond.

The tractor hits the water with a great splash. The engine makes a loud noise, then it stops with a hiss.

Ted climbs down from the tractor.

Ted paddles through the water and out of the pond.
Poppy and Sam run down the hill.
56

Ted is very wet.

Ted takes off his boots and tips out the water.
How can he get the tractor out of the pond?

"Go and ask Farmer Dray to help."

"Ask your mum to telephone Farmer Dray," says Ted. Poppy and Sam run off to the house.
58

Farmer Dray has a big horse.

Soon he walks down the hill with his horse.
It is a huge cart horse, called Dolly.

Ted helps with the ropes.

Farmer Dray ties the ropes to the horse. Ted ties the other ends to the tractor.

Dolly pulls and pulls.

Very slowly the tractor starts to move. Ted pushes as hard as he can and Dolly pulls.

Ted falls over.

The tractor jerks forward and Ted falls in the
water. Now he is wet and muddy all over.

The tractor is out of the pond.

"Better leave the tractor to dry," says Farmer Dray.
"Then you can get the engine going again."

Poppy and Sam ride home.

Farmer Dray lifts them on to Dolly's back.
But Ted is so muddy, he has to walk.

PIG GETS LOST

This is Apple Tree Farm.

This is Mrs Boot, the farmer. She has two children
called Poppy and Sam, and a dog called Rusty.

Mrs Boot has six pigs.

There is a mother pig and five baby pigs. The
smallest pig is called Curly. They live in a pen.

Mrs Boot feeds the pigs every morning.

She takes them two big buckets of food.
But where is Curly? He is not in the pen.

She calls Poppy and Sam.

"Curly has got out," she says. "Please come and help me to find him."

"Where are you, Curly?"

Poppy and Sam call to Curly. "Let's look in the
hen run," says Mrs Boot. But Curly is not there.

70

"There he is, in the barn."

"He's in the barn," says Sam. "I can just see his tail." They all run into the barn to catch Curly.

71

"That's not Curly."

"It's only a piece of rope," says Mrs Boot. "Not Curly's tail." "Where can he be?" says Poppy.
72

"Let's look in the cow shed."

But Curly is not in the cow shed. "Don't worry,"
says Mrs Boot. "We'll soon find him."

"Perhaps he's in the garden."

They look all round the garden but Curly is not there. "I think he's lost for ever," says Sam.

74

"Why is Rusty barking?"

Rusty is standing by a ditch. He barks and barks.
"He's trying to tell us something," says Poppy.

"Rusty has found Curly."

They all look in the ditch. Curly has slipped down into the mud and can't climb out again.

"We'll have to lift him out."

"I'll get into the ditch," says Mrs Boot. "I'm coming too," says Poppy. "And me," says Sam.

Curly is very muddy.

Mrs Boot picks Curly up but he struggles. Then he slips back into the mud with a splash.

78

Now everyone is very muddy.

Sam tries to catch Curly but he falls into the mud.
Mrs Boot grabs Curly and climbs out of the ditch.

They all climb out of the ditch.

"We all need a good wash," says Mrs Boot.
"Rusty found Curly. Clever dog," says Sam.

THE HUNGRY DONKEY

This is Apple Tree Farm.

This is Mrs Boot, the farmer. She has two children called Poppy and Sam, and a dog called Rusty.

There is a donkey on the farm.

The donkey is called Ears. She lives in a field with lots of grass, but she is always hungry.

Ears, the donkey, is going out.

Poppy and Sam catch Ears and take her to the farmyard. Today is the day of the Show.

Ears has a little cart.

They brush her coat, comb her tail and clean her
feet. Mrs Boot puts her into her little cart.

Off they go to the Show.

Poppy and Sam climb up into the little cart. They all go down the lane to the show ground.
86

"You stay here, Ears."

At the show ground, Mrs Boot ties Ears to a
fence. "Stay here. We'll be back soon," she says.

Ears gets free.

Ears is hungry and bored with nothing to do. She pulls and pulls on the rope until she is free.

88

Ears looks for food.

Ears trots across the field to the show ring. She sees a bunch of flowers and some fruit.

"That looks good to eat."

She takes a big bite, but the flowers do not taste very nice. A lady screams and Ears is frightened.

90

Ears runs away.

Mrs Boot, Poppy and Sam and the lady run after her and catch her. "Naughty donkey," says Sam.

Ears is in disgrace.

"I'm sorry," Mrs Boot says to the lady. "Would you like to take Ears into the best donkey competition?"

Ears is very good now.

The lady is called Mrs Rose. She climbs into the cart. "Come on," she says and shakes the reins.

Ears trots into the show ring.

She trots round the ring, pulling the cart. She stops and goes when Mrs Rose tells her.

Ears wins a prize.

"Well done," says the judge and gives her a rosette. He gives Mrs Rose a prize too. It is a hat.

It is time to go home.

Mrs Rose waves goodbye. "That was such fun,"
she says. Ears trots home. She has a new hat too.

SCARECROW'S SECRET

This is Apple Tree Farm.

This is Mrs Boot, the farmer. She has two children, called Poppy and Sam, and a dog called Rusty.

Mr Boot is working in the barn.

"What are you doing, Dad?" asks Sam. "I'm tying lots of straw on these poles," says Mr Boot.

"What is it?"

"You'll soon see," says Dad. "Go and get my old coat from the shed, please. Bring my old hat too."

"It's going to be a scarecrow."

Poppy and Sam come back with the coat and hat.
Then they help Mr Boot put them on the scarecrow.

"He's just like a nice old man."

"I've got some old gloves for him," says Sam.
"Let's call him Mr Straw," says Poppy.

"He's finished now."

"Help me carry him, please, Poppy," says Mr
Boot. "You bring the spade, Sam."

They all go to the corn field.

Mr Boot digs a hole in the field. Then he pushes the pole in so that Mr Straw stands up.

"He does look real."

"I'm sure Mr Straw will scare off all the birds,"
says Sam. "Especially the crows," says Poppy.

Mr Straw is doing a good job.

Every day Mr Boot, Poppy and Sam look at Mr Straw. There are no birds in the corn field.

"There's Farmer Dray's scarecrow."

"He's no good at all," says Sam. "The birds are eating all the corn and standing on the scarecrow."

"Why is Mr Straw so good?"

"Sometimes he looks as if he is moving," says
Poppy. "His coat goes up and down. It's very odd."
108

"Let's go and look."

"Let's creep up very quietly," says Sam. And they tiptoe across the corn field to look at Mr Straw.

"There's something inside his coat."

"It's moving about," says Poppy. "And it's making a funny noise. What is it?" says Sam.
110

"It's our cat and her kittens."

Carefully they open the coat. There is Whiskers, the cat, and two baby kittens hiding in the straw.

"So that's scarecrow's secret."

"Whiskers is helping Mr Straw to frighten off the birds," says Poppy. "Clever Mr Straw," says Sam.

TRACTOR IN TROUBLE

This is Apple Tree Farm.

This is Mrs Boot, the farmer. She has two children, called Poppy and Sam, and a dog called Rusty.
114

Ted works on the farm.

He helps Mrs Boot. Ted looks after the tractor and all the farm machines.

Today it is very windy.

The wind is blowing the trees about and it is very cold. Poppy and Sam play in the barn.

"Where are you going, Ted?"

Ted is driving the tractor out of the yard. "I'm just going to see if the sheep are all right," he says.

Ted stops the tractor by the gate.

He goes into the sheep field. He nails down the roof of the sheep shed to make it safe.

118

Poppy and Sam hear a terrible crash.

"What's that?" says Sam. "I don't know. Let's go and look," says Poppy. They run down the field.

"A tree has been blown down."

"It's come down on Ted's tractor," says Poppy.
"Come on. We must help him," says Sam.
120

"What are you going to do, Ted?"

Poor Ted is very upset. The tree has scratched his new tractor. He can't even get into the cab.

"Ask Farmer Dray to help."

"Go and ask your Mum to phone Farmer Dray,"
says Ted. Poppy and Sam run to the house.

Soon Farmer Dray comes with his horse.

Farmer Dray has a lovely big carthorse, called Dolly. They have come to help Ted.

"I'll cut up the tree first."

Farmer Dray starts up his chain saw. Then he cuts off the branches which have fallen on the tractor.

124

Dolly starts to work.

Farmer Dray ties two ropes to Dolly's harness.
Ted ties the other ends to the big branches.

Dolly pulls and pulls.

She works hard until all the branches are off the tractor. "Well done, Dolly," says Farmer Dray.

126

Ted climbs up into the cab.

"Thank you very much, Farmer Dray and Dolly," he says. And they all go back to the farmyard.

The tractor looks a bit of a mess.

Ted finds a brush and paints over all the scratches.
"It will soon be as good as new," he says.

First published in 1991 by Usborne Publishing Ltd, Usborne House, 83-85 Saffron Hill, London EC1N 8RT, England. Copyright © 1991 Usborne Publishing Ltd.

The name Usborne and the device 🐝 are Trade Marks of Usborne Publishing Ltd. All rights reserved. No part of this publication may be reproduced, stored in a retrieval system or transmitted by any form or by any means, electronic, mechanical, photocopy, recording or otherwise, without the prior permission of the publisher.
Printed in Portugal.